For Sam and Willa and Sandy
And for all our sweet mornings together
—A.S.

To Jonanna, who makes mornings sunnier
—T.H.

Library of Congress Cataloging-in-Publication Data ✦ Stevens, April. ✦ Waking up Wendell / April Stevens ; illustrated by Tad Hills. ✦ 1st ed. ✦ p. cm. ✦ Summary: Early in the morning, a bird begins to sing at #1 Fish Street, waking the man next door and his dog, and before long, as one noise leads to another, everyone on the street is awake. ✦ ISBN 978-0-375-83621-3 (trade) — ISBN 978-0-375-93893-1 (lib. bdg.) [1. Morning—Fiction. 2. Noise—Fiction. 3. Neighborhood—Fiction.] I. Hills, Tad, ill. II. Title. ✦ PZ7.S84315Wak 2007 ✦ [E]—dc22 ✦ 2006030979

PRINTED IN CHINA
2 4 6 8 10 9 7 5 3 1
First Edition

The text of this book is set in Filosofia.

The illustrations are rendered in oil paint and colored pencil.

Written by April Stevens

Illustrated by Tad Hills

Waking Up Wendell

schwartz & wade books new york

Early in the morning, a little bird at #1 Fish
Street hops out of her nest, takes a deep breath,
and begins to sing a very loud and whistley song.

TWEEET

...ta-ta-ta-TWEEEEEET!

At #2 Fish Street, Mr. Krudwig, owner of Krudwig's Bicycle Shop, is in bed dreaming of pancakes.

"Oh, for crying out loud!" Mr. Krudwig grumbles to his dog, Leopold. "That screeching sparrow could wake a brick wall." He climbs out of bed, puts on his checkered bathrobe, and creaks down his stairs to let old Leopold out the back door.

Leopold is happy to be
outside on such a nice day.

Rappity-rappity-

He trots over to his favorite pear tree, makes his morning wee-wee,
then does what he always does first thing. He begins to bark.

No one is quite sure why Leopold does this. Maybe he's shouting
good morning to the other dogs on the street. Maybe he's ordering that
annoying bird to put a lid on it. But whatever the reason, he stands,
wags his little tail, and barks.

All this racket wakes up Mrs. Musky at #3 Fish Street. She opens her bedroom window, leans out, and yells,

"LEOPOLD, YOU STOP THAT YAPPING!"

Then she shuffles into her
kitchen, puts a kettle of water on,
and heads into her bathroom to
get her hair under control.

While she is brushing and spraying
and smoothing, the whistle on Mrs.
Musky's kettle starts to blow high and
clear, like a train pulling out of a station.

WHOOOOOOOOWEEEEEE!

The howling kettle makes Mrs. Depolo at #4 Fish Street sit straight up in bed and blink at the clock. Mrs. Depolo teaches kindergarten and is always late.

"OH, FIDDLEFISH!" she hollers.

She jumps out of bed, throws on her clothes,

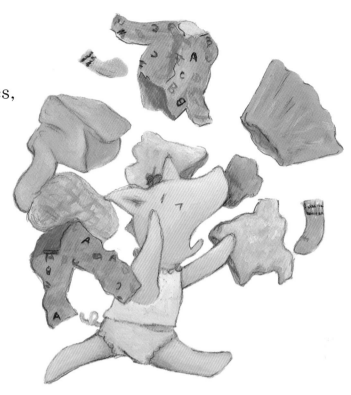

races down her stairs,

and dives out the door.

And as she backs her car out of the driveway, her tires make a loud SCREEEECH! and then a GLEEEEEEP! and then she is gone. Flying down Fish Street!

SCREEEECH!

GLEEEEEP!

The SCREECH! GLEEP! makes Henry Whittlespoon roll over in his bed and yawn. Henry is nine years old and lives at #5 Fish Street. For his birthday his grandma gave him a shiny new harmonica, and since then he plays whenever he can.

So the first thing he does, even before he opens his eyes, is reach under his pillow, pull out his harmonica, and begin to play.

From her bedroom, Mrs. Whittlespoon yells,

"Henry Hobart Whittlespoon! Quit that racket . . .

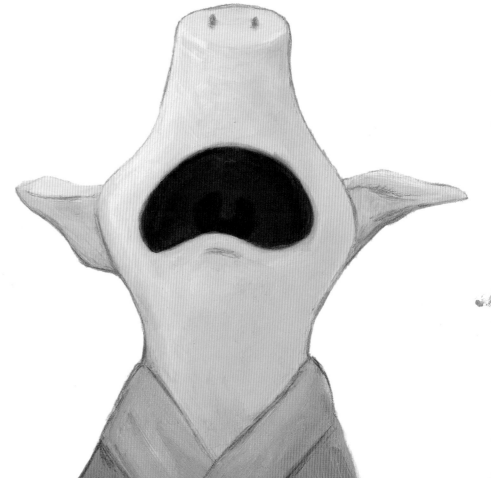

... right this second!"

Henry can't hear her.
But Gloria, who has been sleeping on the doorstep outside
#6 Fish Street, can. She is the Darjeelings' cat, and she uncurls
herself, stands up, and stretches. Thinking of her bowl of kitty
krunchies inside, she pit-pats over to the kitchen door.

Gloria digs her claws into the screen and pulls the door open a little, then lets it go.

WACK-SLAM!

She slips her claws back in and does it again.

WACK-SLAM!

And again—

WACK-SLAM!

Of course this wakes all seven members of the Darjeeling family.

WHOSE
BED
IS IT
ANYWAY?

TRAIN YOUR CAT

WACK-SLAM!

It also wakes Marjorie Parks at
#7 Fish Street. Marjorie has been
sewing a wedding dress straight
through the night and has just dozed off
at her sewing machine.

One WACK-SLAM! of the Darjeelings' door and she
jerks awake. She blinks sleepily at the silky white dress
and remembers she needs to get it finished—now!

Marjorie puts her foot to the pedal, PLUNK, and up starts her sewing machine. First slowly,

wug-a-ta-

wug-a-ta-

wug-a-ta-

wug-a-ta

then building up speed as she loudly finishes the final seam.

Wigata-wigata-wigata...

. . . wigata-wigata

Old Mr. Wink at #8 Fish Street has been trying to wake up for a while. When Mrs. Parks's machine starts up next door, he forces himself out of bed. He moves slowly, like honey pouring from a jar.

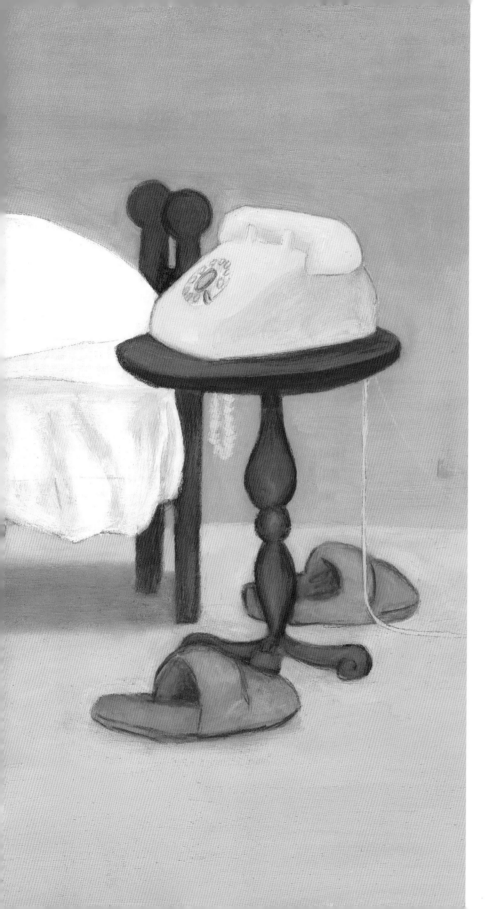

He stands, puts his left blue slipper
on, then sits back down.

After three more yawns and one more
blue slipper, he picks up his telephone
and calls Lilah Hall at #9 Fish Street.

RING!
RING-RING-RING!

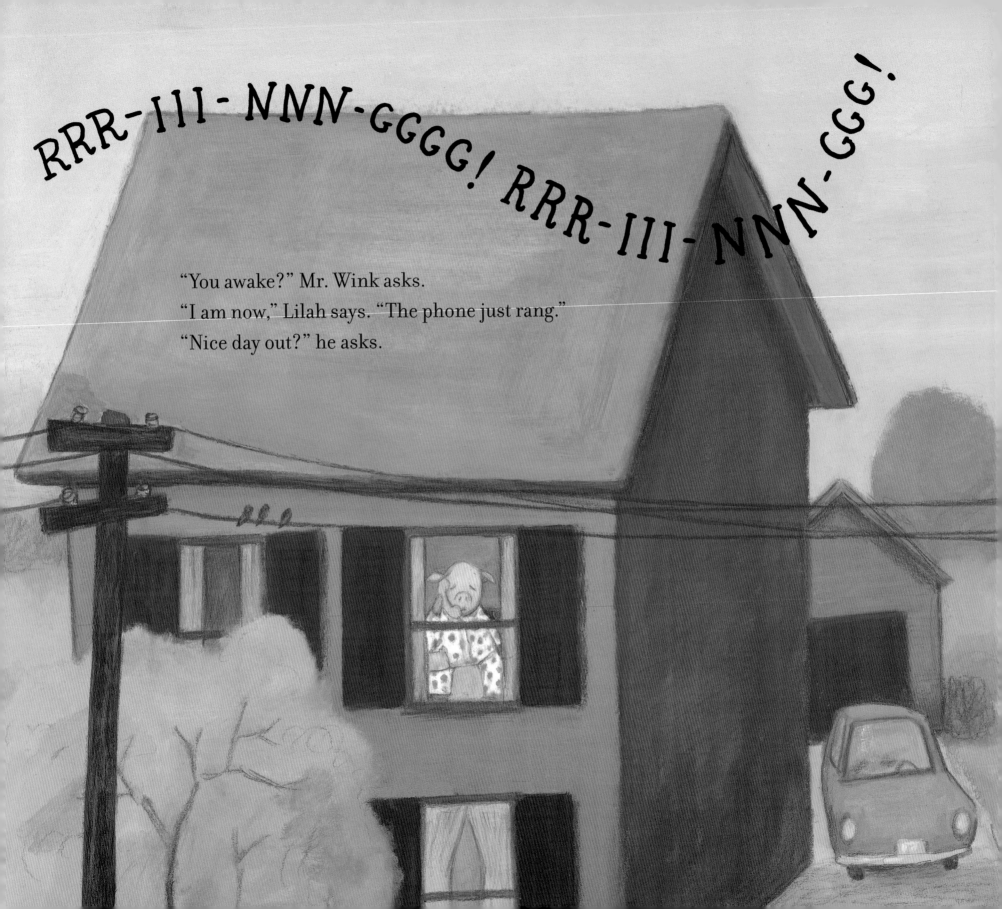

RRR-III-NNN-GGGG! RRR-III-NNN-GGG!

"You awake?" Mr. Wink asks.

"I am now," Lilah says. "The phone just rang."

"Nice day out?" he asks.

Lilah leans over and looks out her window. "Sun's singing and the birds are shining. I mean, sun's shining and the birds are singing. Looks lovely, Mr. Wink."

"Well, just called to see if you were up," says Mr. Wink, and he takes off his blue slippers and lies back down. A few minutes later, he's snoring like a chain saw.

After Lilah hangs up, she steps right into her shower and starts to sing. And Lilah Hall can really sing.

Lilah sings so loud and so high that all the birds on Fish Street stop their own singing, "TWEEEEET-TA-TA . . . ," and tilt their little heads to listen.

"Oh, isn't it

grand! Isn't it fine! To be here with you . . .

. . . in the sunshine!"

And it is Lilah's song that finally wakes the last person on Fish Street who is still asleep. He lives at #10, and when he hears these beautiful high notes, he opens his eyes.

Hanging above him is a mobile with lots of little blue and red and green birds floating through the air. He looks up at these and makes a squeal of happiness.

That's when his mother comes in and
lifts him up so he's also in the air.

"Well, Wendell Willamore,

my little bird," she sings,

"finally you are awake!"